THE SNOWMAN the animated film is available on Polygram video
THE SNOWMAN is a TVC London production
director DIANNE JACKSON supervising director JIMMY MURAKAMI
producer JOHN COATES executive producer IAIN HARVEY
music and lyrics by HOWARD BLAKE

A catalogue record for this book is available
from the British Library

Published by Ladybird Books Ltd Loughborough Leicestershire UK
Ladybird Books Ltd is a subsidiary of the Penguin Group of companies
LADYBIRD and the device of a Ladybird are trademarks of Ladybird Books Ltd
© SNOWMAN ENTERPRISES LTD MCMLXXXVIII
This edition published MCMXCVI

Raymond Briggs'
The
Snowman™

Ladybird

The Snowman

It was morning and as soon as
he opened his eyes and saw the
bright, white light coming
through the window,

James knew it would be a
magical day…

It was **SNOWING!**

He'd never dressed so quickly. Hardly time for breakfast!

At *last* he was outside making giant footprints in the snow and throwing snowballs.

He began to roll a huge snowball and suddenly had an idea. The *best* thing to do would be to make a... SNOWMAN.

A big , big body.

A quick lunch – no time to stop!

A big round head.

Coal eyes, a tangerine nose, a hat and scarf and last of all... James drew a mouth with his finger.

His snowman was finished.

His snowman was *smiling!*

Soon it was time for bed...

but it's hard to sleep when you're thinking of a snowman outside, all alone.

James got up and went out into the night. The day had been special...

but *this* was magical.
The snowman waved,
raised his hat

and walked
towards
the house.

James took the snowman's hand
and they went indoors.

Ordinary snowmen *never* go inside a house but *this* snowman wanted to see everything.

The 'fridge was best – it was cold, just how snowmen like it! Upstairs, Mum and Dad were fast asleep.

The snowman tried everything – including Mum's perfume, which nearly made him... sneeze!

The snowman danced to a music box

and played with James's toys.
Mum and Dad didn't wake up.

Back outside they rode through the fields and forests on Dad's motorbike...

But the snowman needed to be cold and the motorbike made his legs very hot.

So James took the snowman to the big freezer and soon ...the snowman's legs were mended.

Then suddenly
the snowman
stopped smiling
and listened.

What could
he hear? Was he
remembering
something?

Then he began to run across
the snow. James ran
with him. He caught
the snowman's
hand and...
all at once...
they
were
walking
in the
air...

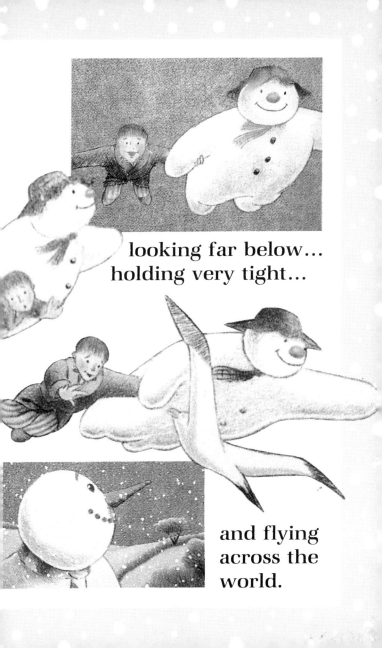

looking far below...
holding very tight...

and flying
across the
world.

When at last they landed, the snowman led James through dark, dark woods...

until they came upon the most amazing sight that James could ever have imagined.

All the snowmen and snow-women in the world had come for a party!

And there was Father Christmas!
He gave James a present
– and a hug.

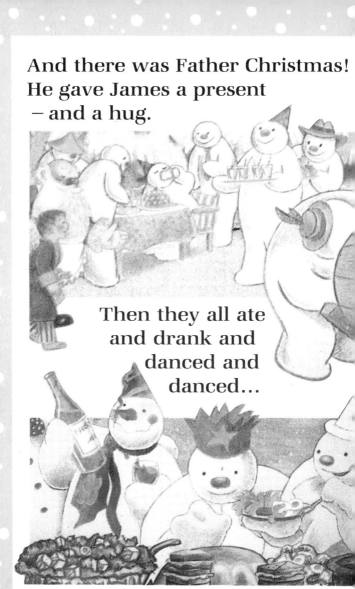

Then they all ate
and drank and
danced and
danced...

and danced...

until it was time to go home.

They
flew
back the
same way they
had come...

and soon they landed safely in James's garden.

The snowman stood where James had first made him

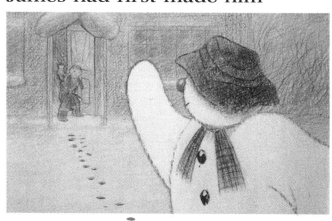

but then
James ran back,
gave him
one last hug...

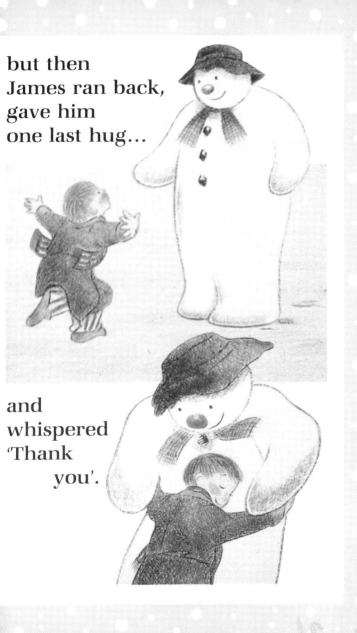

and
whispered
'Thank
     you'.

Next morning the sun was shining. James leapt out of bed – rushed down the stairs and out through the door to see his very special snowman.

He couldn't believe his eyes as he walked towards a heap of melted snow, and a hat, a scarf, a tangerine and some pieces of coal.

Had he been dreaming?

James felt in his dressing gown pocket and pulled out a snowman scarf – his present, given to him by Father Christmas, far away on one magical night.